In My Grandmother's Garden

A **MUSICTALE**© *with music and lyrics*
by Kit Eakle

Best wishes,
Jean Eakle

Enjoy!
Kit Eakle

Illustrations
by Jean Eakle

with Aubyn Eakle

A **MUSICTALE**©
by **MUSICKIT**
778 Western Dr., Point Richmond, CA, 94801
www.musickit.com

Hi! My name is Aubyn.
This book is a true story about me and my grandmother. When I was younger, my grandparents would take care of me at their house when my parents couldn't be home with me. Some of my happiest moments were spent in my grandma's garden planting or picking flowers.

When my father came to get me I was often asleep. Driving home, I'd dream half-waking dreams of the day. My head and heart are still full of memories of those times.

I remember picking flowers to make little bouquets in tiny doll vases. We would set up a stand in the garden and pretend to sell them to imaginary customers. As there were no real customers, we gave all the bouquets to Grandpa. Sometimes Grandma and I painted our bouquets. We gave the paintings to Grandpa too.

Grandpa passed away several years ago. Yet it seems like only yesterday he smiled tenderly as I handed him the bouquets. The flowers have long since faded, but our paintings still remind us of those sunny days. I hope you enjoy them — and the song my uncle Kit says our pictures inspired him to write. Perhaps they will inspire you to make memories of your own.

In my Grandmother's garden, at her home by the bay,

The morning sunshine promised an almost perfect day.

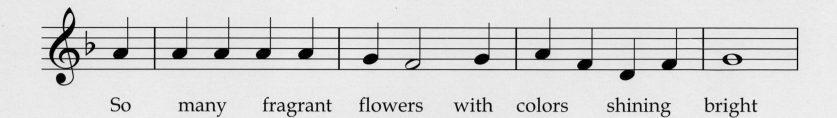

So many fragrant flowers with colors shining bright

All washed clean by the golden sheen of the San Francisco light...

In my grandmother's garden.

As an artist grandma told me her flowers taught her to see.

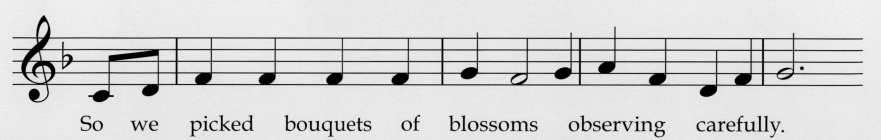

So we picked bouquets of blossoms observing carefully.

As daylight changed their colors, we played with colors too.

While Grandma sat painting me in my hat, I painted every hue...

In my grandmother's garden.

In my Grandmother's garden we painted all afternoon.

Enchanted by flowery visions, our light began to fade too soon.

We brushed the last strokes carefully, and as the wet paint dried,

I looked with awe at all she saw with new eyes opened wide...

In my grandmother's garden.

As the day turned towards evening, just before the sun had set,

We showed grandpa our flowers, though the petals were still wet.

Grandpa smiled so tenderly, I climbed into his lap...

Now Grandpa's gone, but I still dream on in my mem'ries of that nap...

In my grandmother's garden.

In my Grandmother's garden shadows stole the light.

The evening sunlight faded turning daylight into night

My Papa woke me saying, "My love, it's time to go."

That day has gone, but tomorrow the sun will shine again, I know...

And my heart still burns with all I learned from her wise eyes long ago

In my Grandmother's garden

In My Grandmother's Garden

For more information see
http://www.musickit.com
or contact: kit@musickit.com

"I love you Grandma." - "I love you Aubyn."

The publisher/author wishes to acknowledge all those who have given their help and support creating this book including: Peggy Geary; Lucia Eakle, Juanita Newland-Ulloa and her daughter, Cristina; Ellen Troyer and family; all the kids at Reed Elementary School; Eduardo and everyone at Craft Press; Laurie Lewis, Matt Eakle, John Burr, Alex Baum for their music; all the music educators and teachers I have worked with over the years, especially my friends at OAKE and KSC; but most of all to my mother, Jean, and niece, Aubyn Rose, who let me tell their story.

Library of Congress Cataloging-in-Publication data
Eakle, Kit; Eakle, Laura Jean
In my grandmother's garden/ Music and lyrics by Kit Eakle, illustrations by Laura Jean Eakle—1st ed. • [32]p. :col. ill. ; cm.
Summary:
A young girl tells a true story in music about how her grandmother shared her love of flowers and painting, and how it helped them both deal with the death of the girls grandfather.
ISBN 0-9655451-4-8   LC Control Number 2001 126617
1. Music. 2. Art — painting — watercolor. 3. Gardening — flowers.
I. Title

II. Eakle, Kit
01 126617

In My Grandmother's Garden

by Kit Eakle

In my grandmother's garden, at her home by the Bay, the morning sunshine promised an almost perfect day. So

many fragrant flowers, with colors shining bright... All washed clean by the golden sheen of the San Francisco light... In my grandmother's garden.

Verse 2:
As an artist grandma told me her flowers taught her to see
So we picked bouquets of blossoms observing carefully.
As daylight changed their colors we played with colors too.
While grandma sat painting me in my hat,
I painted every hue in my grandmother's garden.

Verse 3:
In my grandmother's garden we painted all afternoon
Enchanted by flowery visions our light faded all to soon.
We brushed the last strokes carefully and as the wet paint dried,
I looked with awe at all she saw
with new eyes opened wide in my grandmothers garden.

Verse 4:
As the day turned towards evening, just before the sun had set,
We showed grandpa our flowers though the petals were still wet.
Grandpa smiled so tenderly, I climbed into his lap.
Now grandpa's gone, but I still dream on
In my memories of that nap in my grandmother's garden.

Verse 5:
In my grandmother's garden shadows stole the light.
The evening sunlight faded turning daylight into night.
My papa woke me saying, "My love it's time to go."
That day has gone but tomrrow the sun will shine again I know.
And my heart still burnes from all I learned from those wise eyes long ago...
In my grandmother's garden.